In the Snow: Who's Been Here?

LINDSAY BARRETT GEORGE

Greenwillow Books, New York

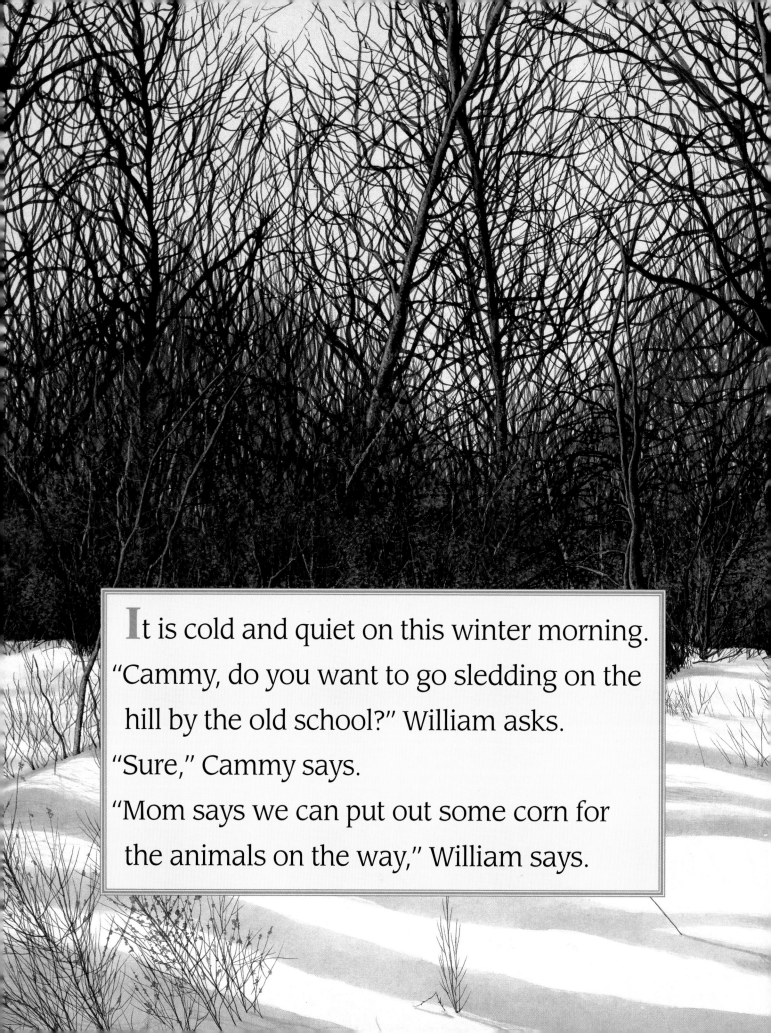

It is cold and quiet on this winter morning.
"Cammy, do you want to go sledding on the
hill by the old school?" William asks.
"Sure," Cammy says.
"Mom says we can put out some corn for
the animals on the way," William says.

The children walk up the lane and cross the township road.

They follow an old trail into the woods. Cammy stops to throw corn on the ground. William sees tracks between some barberry bushes.

Who's been here?

A ruffed
grouse.

William and Cammy hike up a small hill.

They hear a bird's song.

Whoit! Whoit! Whoit!

The children reach a clearing in the woods.

The bird is gone.

Fuzzy red balls sprinkle the snow under

a clump of sumac.

Who's been here?

A cardinal.

The trail winds along the frozen pond.
William and his sister look up into the
branches of an old oak tree.
They see a leafy nest.

Who's been here?

A family of
gray squirrels.

The children pass a hemlock tree.
Freshly cut and gnawed branches
lie at the bottom of the tree.
But there are no footprints.

Who's been here?

A porcupine.

"Let's put the rest of the corn under that white pine tree," Cammy says.
They spread the corn and find a pellet of feathers and bones at the base of the tree.

Who's been here?

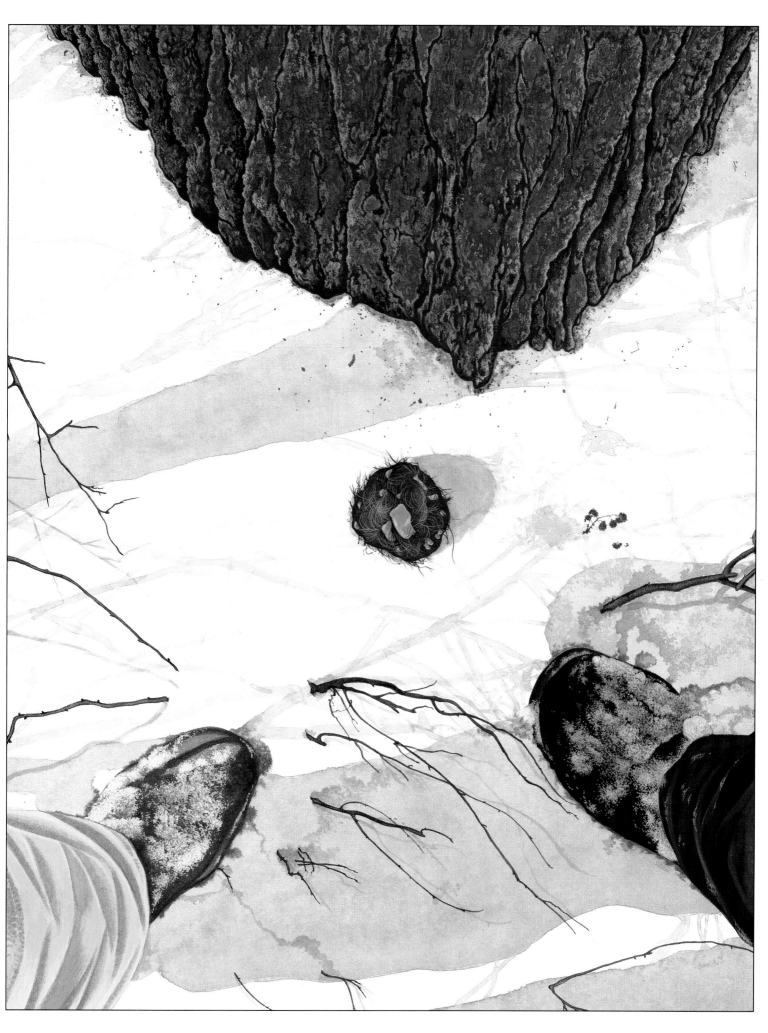

A great
horned owl.

William stops the toboggan.

He sees a small hole in the snow.

It is the entrance to a tunnel.

Broken acorn shells surround the hole.

Who's been here?

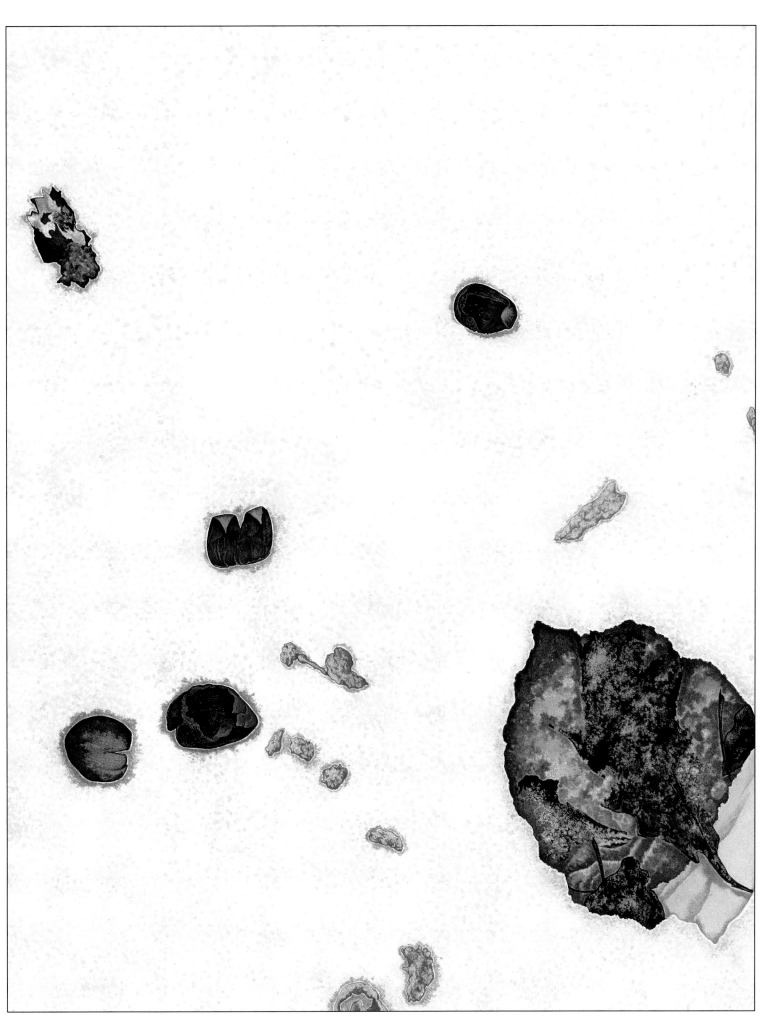

A chipmunk.

William and Cammy follow the trail down to the brook.
They see tracks going in and out of the water.
William finds a fish head on the bank.

Who's been here?

A mink
and a trout.

A clump of birch trees grows along the trail. A patch of bark has been rubbed off one of the trees.

Who's been here?

A buck.

The trail passes through a gate in a stone wall and ends in an open field at the top of the hill.

"We're here," William says, "and it's a long way down."

Cammy finds a toboggan with a thermos of hot chocolate, three cups, and some doughnuts.

"I wonder who's been here?" she asks.

But William knows. . . .

The **ruffed grouse** is a plump bird with short wings. Its flight is quick and erratic. Grouse like to live in overgrown fields with shrubs and woods nearby. They eat insects, berries, seeds, leaves, and buds. During the winter, barberries are a favorite food because the berries' high oil content helps the grouse maintain its body temperature.

The **great horned owl** lives in heavily wooded areas. It hunts at night and feeds mostly on small animals. The owl is a good hunter, with keen night vision and extra-sensitive hearing, and it flies almost noiselessly. It swallows its prey whole—flesh, bones, and hair—and later spits up pellets, or balls, made up of everything that could not be digested.

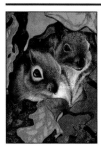

The **cardinal** is a shy bird that likes open fields next to thickets or evergreen trees. It has a strong beak, which is used for cracking open seeds and pits. Both the male and female cardinal guard their home territory all year long. The male cardinal's feathers are much brighter than the female's.

The **chipmunk** is a small member of the squirrel family. Chipmunks like to eat nuts, seeds, and fruit. They spend the winter in vast systems of underground tunnels. On a warm winter day, this chipmunk has taken acorns to the surface to eat in the sun.

Gray squirrels make their winter homes in the tops of tall trees. They love to eat acorns and other nuts, seeds, and berries. Squirrels prepare for winter by burying nuts and seeds in holes that they dig in the ground. If they forget where their food is hidden, trees often will sprout from the undiscovered spots.

The **mink** spends most of its life swimming or running through streams and the edges of lakes and ponds. It is active at night and is seldom seen by humans. Minks like to eat small animals, birds, eggs, frogs, and fish. The trout is a favorite food because of its tiny scales, which make it easier to eat, and its high fat content, which helps the mink stay warm in winter.

The **porcupine** spends the winter in the tops of trees. It prefers heavily wooded areas, particularly those where evergreens grow. For food, the porcupine strips bark from tree trunks and branches. It is very slow moving, but its sharp quills protect it from other animals.

In the fall, this **buck** (male deer) rubs the bark from a young birch tree to mark its territory. Marking helps to keep other bucks away and to attract does (female deer). Sometimes a buck will also stab a sapling with its horns as practice for future fights.

For Libby, who encouraged me first

Special thanks to George Holtzapple, Liz Lewis, Jan Rethorst from the Delaware Valley Raptor Center, Janine Weiss, and my husband, Bill

Gouache paints were used for the full-color art.
The text type is Usherwood Medium.

Library of Congress Cataloging-in-Publication Data
George, Lindsay Barrett.

In the snow: who's been here?/ by Lindsay Barrett George.
    p.   cm.   "Greenwillow Books."
Summary: Two children on their way to go sledding see evidence of a variety of animal life.
ISBN 0-688-12320-1 (trade)   ISBN 0-688-12321-X (lib. bdg.)
ISBN 0-688-17056-0 (paper)
[1. Winter—Fiction.   2. Animal tracks—Fiction.]
I.Title.   PZ7.G29334In   1995   [E]—dc20
94-20842   CIP   AC

10 9 8   First Edition